WORRIES

FEARS

FRUSTRATIONS

DOUBTS

WHEN THINGS AREN'T GOING RIGHT,

GO LEFT

Words by MARC COLAGIOVANNI

Art by PETER H. REYNOLDS

ORCHARD BOOKS · NEW YORK · AN IMPRINT of SCHOLASTIC INC.

One day,
for no particular reason,
nothing was going right.

Absolutely,
positively,
NOTHING
was going right.

So...
I decided to
go left.

The first thing I did?
I left behind
my worries.

Yup! I left them
right there on the ground.

They looked up at me and wondered,
"Where are you going?"

But I just smiled and
waved goodbye.
"Wait!"
they hollered.
"Come back!
What will happen to us?"

I simply shrugged my shoulders,
"You'll be fine."

As I walked away, I thought —

Did I make the right choice?

Should I go back
and get them?

Doubts crept in.

So you know what I did?

I left behind my doubts.
Yup! I left them right there
on the ground.

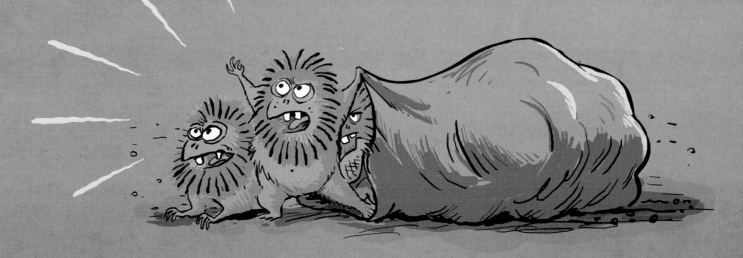

They bellowed,
"You're making a mistake!"

But I just gazed at the sky.

They questioned,
"Are you sure you're making
the right decision?"

"Absolutely!"
I declared.

With my worries
and doubts left behind,
I could finally think clearly.

I forged on until I came to a pool
and a diving board I remembered all too well.

The last time I tried to dive off that diving board,
I splatted on my back—ouch!

So you know what I did?

I left behind my fears.

Yup!

I left them right there on the ground.

I stood up straight,
shoulders back,
hands pressed above
my head.

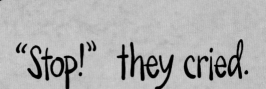

"Stop!" they cried.
But I simply turned and gave them a wink.

I leaped!

SPLAT!

On my back, once again,
oof, that stings.

I thought to myself, *This is impossible!*
It can't be done!

So you know what I did?

I left behind my frustrations.
Yup! I left them
right there on the ground.

They yelled,
"You can't do it!"

I whispered to myself, "No way. Never."

I leaped!

Feet together, toes pointed, legs straight,

PERFECT.

I did it!

I started to realize, the more left I went, the more right I felt!

So you know what I did?

Yup! I kept going left!

And before I knew it —
EVERYTHING was going right!

As I walked home,
I glanced at the ground, and I
noticed something that I did not expect!

My frustrations were a lot smaller.

My fears, a lot quieter.

My doubts, a lot calmer.

My worries, practically gone!

So ... I decided to pick them back up.

And you know what?
They felt lighter now.
And they weren't so hard to handle anymore.

And I realized,
it was okay to have them with me,
so long as I kept an eye on them.

And made sure that they didn't get too big.

Or too loud. Or too overwhelming.

But if they did, and I felt like nothing was going right again? Then I'd simply...

...go left.

When life's burdens
start to feel
too heavy…

don't be afraid
to put them down
for a while.

—MARC COLAGIOVANNI

to Lauren, Addison, Ella, and Mia.
— M.C.

to Tom Snyder — a master teacher,
an out-of-box thinker, and my mentor
who invited me to change the world.
— P.H.R.

Text Copyright © 2023 by Marc Colagiovanni • Illustrations Copyright © 2023 by Peter H. Reynolds

All rights reserved. Published by Orchard Books, an imprint of Scholastic Inc., *Publishers since 1920.* ORCHARD BOOKS and design are registered trademarks of Watts Publishing Group, Ltd., used under license. SCHOLASTIC and associated logos are trademarks and/or registered trademarks of Scholastic Inc.

Library of Congress Cataloging-in-Publication Data Available

ISBN 978-1-338-83118-4

10 9 8 7 6 5 4 3 2 1   23 24 25 26 27

Printed in China   38
First edition, March 2023
The text type and display are hand-lettered by Peter H. Reynolds.
Reynolds Studio assistance by John Lechner
Book design by Doan Buu and Patti Ann Harris